A WOMAN'S BODY

OKUHLE ESETHU

OE PUBLICATIONS

First published in South Africa in 2024 by

OE Publications

Copyright © Lindokuhle Esethu Hlatshwayo, 2024

ISBN: 978-0-7961-9365-0

For more information visit: www.oepublications.com

A WOMAN'S BODY

CONTENTS

a woman's body is supposed to be
a private space.
an altar.

but what happens when
the body
is turned into
a human excretion site?
an ornament?
an object put on shelves to be picked by men?
a victim of harassment and violation,
constantly subjected to humiliation
and degradation?

a woman's body is supposed to be hers,
and only hers, to own.

A DIRTY BODY

What am I supposed to do with all this shame that I feel in my own body?

It's like a clogged sewage pipe where all the waste has been dumped in excess, and now there's no room for clean water to flow.

I feel dirty. I feel dirty in my own body.

It's hard to go on living, loving, dreaming, feeling, when my body is a storage house for trauma.

I get choked by the recollection of my memories of that night. They are heavy on my chest, a bandwagon around my neck.

The thing about traumatic experiences is that they always leave a mark. When something like that happens to you, you can never go back to who you once were. You lose yourself, you lose your identity, you lose your innocence. It hurts to grieve a past self you can never return to being.

Everything is as always, but I'm not.

What do I do with this dirty body?

A DIRTY BODY (PART 2)

My eyes are bloodshot red and throbbing. After wiping the tears off my face, I muster bravery with three deep breaths. I'm still sobbing inside. It hurts. It hurts and it can't stop hurting. The pain I feel makes my body weak and my knees wobbly. Walking is a strenuous exercise, and I wish the detective walking in front of me could pick me up and give me a piggyback ride, the way my mother did when I was a child. My mother, she's not here. I wish she was, but then she would know what has happened to her daughter and I don't want her to know. It would break her. I'm far from home. Too far. Perhaps that is why this has happened…

As soon as we step inside the hospital unit designated for patients like myself, rape victims, I forget that I'm in a hospital. It looks and feels nothing like it, it's more like home. My nostrils are greeted by a comfortably clean scent, which wraps around me in a warm embrace, soothing my senses. The walls are pristine white, devoid of the usual clutter found in hospitals. When we reach the end of the corridor, the detective stops at what is supposed to be a reception, but again, it's too homely for a reception. There's a nurse-receptionist at the desk. She greets us both then I'm ushered into a pink room with a cute couch, a bar fridge and a cupboard stocked with amenities. I sit down on the cute couch while the detective briefs the nurse-receptionist about my case. A TV in front of me, mounted on the wall, playing a familiar show, transports me back to home and for a while I feel the presence of my family offering me solace.

After their exchange by the reception, the detective and nurse-receptionist walk into the pink room. The nurse-receptionist's warm smile exudes gentleness from her kind face. She tells me to make myself comfortable. The detective assures me of my safety in this homely environment. She must leave but promises to come back to pick me up later, once "everything is done".

The kind nurse-receptionist asks if I need anything while I wait for the doctor. "Tea? Water? A sandwich?" But my body can't take in anything, so I say no. Another nurse, also gentle in demeanour and much older than the nurse-receptionist calls me into the doctor's room a few minutes later. Her voice is soft, almost a whisper. She talks to me as if aware of how fragile I am at this moment. Here, I am treated with the kindness I desperately need.

When I step into the doctor's room, a teddy bear catches my eye, and like a child, I instinctively embrace it without asking for permission. My body relaxes as I hug it.
It soothes my inner child. The nurse resembling my gentle grandmother checks my blood pressure and collects samples for tests.

Given a cup for my urine sample, I leave the doctor's room to the bathroom, as I'm peeing it feels as though I'm releasing all the vulgarity of the rape from my system. I don't exactly know how to feel, but for some reason, I'm proud of myself for this. It's liberating to slowly take the power over my body back like this...

Returning to the doctor's room, I am surprised to find a male doctor with the nurse. Why him? Why not a female doctor? Why did they call a man to assist me when I told them it's a man who hurt me, caused all this damage? My mind is racing. I am alarmed and concerned but not angry. But then his demeanour puts me at ease. He is not tense nor soft. He talks to me in a normal doctor's tone, and I realise I need the balance of softness for my inner child and sternness for the young woman I currently am.

So, my walls go down. Not completely, just a bit. I don't think I'll ever trust men…

I cuddle my teddy again while he sets up the rape testing kit. Then what feels like an interrogation starts. He asks questions. Lots of questions. About him. About them. About me. About that night. About how much I had to drink. I try my best to recollect the night, tell him everything, including the fact that I don't remember much. Everything is blurry or blackened. I blacked out!

The doctor emphasises that I should tell him as much as my mind can remember because my stories need to make sense and add up in court, in case I go to court, if I want to press charges.

Pressing charges! That's something I still have to think about. But it's a thought for later; for now, I just want to focus on cleansing my body and beginning the journey to healing…

A DIRTY BODY (PART 3)

Now that I've summoned up the courage to recollect and reflect on the chain of events of that fateful night, I can confirm the demise of my sense of Self and the pollution of my innocence. A first date. A glass of wine. Heavy braids torn from the scalp. Dress and heels thrust on the floor. Cigarette smoke stinging my face. Ripped lace underwear. A swollen face. Bleeding thighs.

Where to begin?
The first date or the bleeding thighs?
The moment of deception or the moment of violation?

The beginning.
It was on a Sunday afternoon when he texted me to ask if I had any plans for the evening.
I did. But I was willing to cancel them to finally see him for the first time. Weeks of phone conversations after connecting on a dating app had built up anticipation.

"No. I don't have any plans. Why?" (15:03)
I replied to his text.
"Wanna take you out and spoil you." (15:50)
He initiated.

Three hours later, I was in an Uber he had requested for me, headed to a fancy restaurant boasting a sea view. I am a simple girl, was. I don't know what I am now except a dirty body with gnawing thoughts (an anxious mind) and overwhelming emotions (a guilt-ridden heart). I couldn't even pronounce the name of the restaurant. My inferiority complex emerged from its hiding place when I saw the interior of the restaurant. It wasn't a place I had ever dreamt of even dining in. Doubt crept in as I entered, feeling out of place. The guy seemed leagues above my standard, intensifying my anxiety and insecurity.

He was not there upon my arrival. After what seemed like a rude forever, he sent a text:
"On the way, sweetheart. Order something in the meantime." (20:07)

I refrained from ordering, afraid he wouldn't show. Nothing to eat on that menu was within my budget. So, I just kept sipping on the glass of water with lemon the waiter had brought for me upon arrival, instead of dwelling on the embarrassment of being potentially stood-up. Being more than an hour late for a first date sets a tone. It reveals lack of respect and a desire to assert dominance. I didn't reflect on that in that moment, though. I was feeling too nervous and insecure to read between the lines and take note of the already glaring red flags. More than that, I was a patient and overly understanding human being before the incident, which always resulted in me tolerating just about any bullshit anyone tossed my way.

As time dragged on, I became a nervous wreck thinking he had stood me up. But he hadn't. When he finally arrived, he explained that he was late because he had to pick up his friend, whose partner cancelled on him last minute, before the date. Yes! The first date was supposed to be a double date, which I had no knowledge of until I was sitting across two men who were ten years old than me, expressing their disappointment of the other girl's cancellation. Looking back now, I wonder if there was ever the friend's partner in the first place, or I had been intentionally set up by vultures who planned on taking advantage of me later, reducing my body into a thing to play with and to please their whims...

I instantly recognised my date the minute he strode into the restaurant, his T-shirt catching my eye.

<u>"Princess, am here, wearing a white tee and greyish jeans."</u> (20:40)

It wasn't just any T-shirt he wore; it was Gucci, paired with LV jeans and Air Jordan sneakers. As he approached with his companion, I couldn't help by admire his expensive ensemble. I looked down at my cheap black body-con dress and felt painfully out of place. My roommate had insisted it was the perfect first-date attire, flattering and alluring. Yet, when I compared his outfit to mine, I felt like nothing more than an ordinary girl.

"Mbalehle?" He beamed with a smile, flashing his grills when he reached the table I had chosen. Instead of pronouncing my name as MBA-LE-NHLE, his Congolese sounding accent greeted me as MBA-LE-HLE.

"I hope that sounded right," he said softly, with his smile unwavering.

"Hey, yes," I replied with a smile of my own, masking any discomfort I felt at the disparity between our appearances.

"Come on, give me a hug, sweetheart," he coaxed, extending his arms. I rose reluctantly to oblige.
But this was not the standard cordial embrace you give to a person you just met; it was stifling, possessive even.
He clung on longer than etiquette warranted, his grip refusing to loosen, surpassing the mere three seconds customary greeting. Again, a red flag glowed and glared in my eyes, but I took no note of it, opting for politeness over intuition. Throughout this uncomfortable exchange, the friend stood silently on the side. When my date finally released me from his hold, after I had moved my upper body to signal that I wanted to let go, I shook hands with the friend, and we sat down. I brushed aside how uncomfortable and unsafe the hug made me feel and went on with the night.

We spent nearly an hour at dinner, with my date doing most of the talking - about himself, his personal life and his work. He owned a chain of clubs in the city and had other businesses he could not yet disclose because we were still only acquaintances.

Fair, I thought to myself.

I did not expect someone I had just met to give me their life history. But with the way things unfolded later, I wished I had asked more questions to gauge his intentions with me. Yes, he spoke excessively about himself, but I still did not perceive him as a rapist. I only thought that he was a guy who was too self-absorbed to hold a conversation that was not centred around him. It turned out to be worse than what I had assumed. He showed no genuine interest in me as a person; I was merely an object in his eyes. The friend spoke here and there, his quiet nature evident throughout our interaction.

After dinner, two bottles of wine were ordered as dessert. We sipped on the wine with my date still doing much of the talking. Normally, I would keep track of how many glasses I had, but my mind was elsewhere that night. Home, perhaps. I think I was bored but could not admit it. My glass kept getting refilled each time I emptied it until my head felt heavy around my neck. You never realise how drunk you are when you drink while sitting down until you stand up, and by then, it's too late to slow down.

It was when I got up to go to the bathroom that I realised I was too drunk. I should have gone home then. I should have asked him to arrange a ride for me. But I didn't. I blame myself a lot for not making the right decisions that night, for forgetting my limit.

When I returned from the bathroom, our table had been cleared. They both proposed a second location, and unfortunately, I agreed. I deeply regret agreeing to that too. I always will. I regret not being brave enough to firmly say NO to being taken to their house, a territory that tipped the scales and rendered me powerless, made me prey to vultures. I still cannot comprehend my mindset hat night. I was not thinking at all. A second location is never a good idea; it invariably sours the experience of the evening.

The drive back to their place was a blur. I believe I fell asleep at some point in the car, I don't remember at all. I only recall my interaction with the security guard at their estate once we arrived. The security guard asked for my ID and seemed surprised by my age. I think he realised that I was too young to be with men of their age at that hour of the night. I laughed off whatever he had said and followed my hosts to their apartment. I am actually not sure if I followed them, or I was balanced on my date the whole time. However, once we were inside the apartment, I was politely instructed to make myself comfortable. I did, by reclining on the couch with my legs folded. Then I was handed the drink that led to my blackout. It's more difficult to refuse alcohol once you've already exceeded your limit. When you are too intoxicated, you forget your boundaries. The last thing I remember was gulping down my drink... After that, everything became a blur, then darkness.

There are violent and elusive glimpses of that night. Images of cigarette smoke swirling around my face, accompanied by derisive laughter of malicious men, haunt my memory. I believe I was nothing more than a source of amusement to them in that state. I also have flashes of a muscular, naked body looming over mine, with me struggling to push it away before everything fades to black...

When I opened my heavy and painful eyes the next morning, it was to the sight of an unfamiliar ceiling. I felt the presence of two bodies sandwiching me, I looked right then left, pulled up the blankets to look underneath and screamed in horror at my nakedness!

They both woke up suddenly, startled by my screams.

I was overwhelmed with confusion, fear, frustration, and anger. It was painfully obvious what had happened, but I could not remember consenting to it. I still cannot. I was not in the right state of mind to have given consent to such vulgarity…

The worst thing about the rape is not remembering anything at all but waking up with a dirty body.

DOING THINGS DIFFERENTLY
(A DIRTY BODY)

I cannot help but think to myself:

Perhaps if I had done things differently, I would not be where I am today. Perhaps I should not have gone to his place. Perhaps I should have worn jeans rather than that short body-con dress. Perhaps I should not have drunk the wine. Perhaps I should not have laughed at his jokes. Perhaps I should not have flirted with him before, during and briefly after the date. Perhaps I should not have gone on the date. Perhaps I should not have texted back.
Perhaps I should not have been on a dating app.
Perhaps I should not have put myself out there at all.

My therapist says this kind of thinking is what perpetrators count on; they thrive on burdening the blame on the victim. It makes sense what she says, but I still cannot help but look for reasons to blame myself and pin down how I played a role in my own rape. I just cannot help it.

A DIRTY BODY (PART 5)

To heal old wounds, you have to go back to the past and familiarise yourself with it. Make it so familiar that it no longer hurts when you are alone reflecting on it.

I'm not quite there yet. Healing isn't a linear process; it's more like being in a deep pit, trying to climb out. Sometimes you make it halfway up, and other times you almost reach the top, only to spiral back down. I'm often hit by a tsunami of overwhelming emotions that displace me from my sense of self when I think I've moved passed the rape. I now consider myself a survivor rather than a rape victim. "Survivor" feels more fitting because it reflects that I've reclaimed my power over my body. However, that does not mean I've completely forgotten or moved passed what happened. I don't think I'll ever completely get over it. Some wounds leave scars that never fully heal. Some stains are permanent, impossible to wash away.

...

WOMANING

You, Vuyiseka, wore your heart on your sleeves. You dared to reveal the inner workings of your mind in conversation. You spoke openly and freely about everything while we coyly tried to make sense of our womanhood and whispered words like "vagina", "breasts", "sex", "period pains", or found more polite synonyms for them. Becoming fully fledged women frightened most of us, all of us, except you. It wasn't that you particularly enjoyed the experience, but you embraced and honoured it.

Being a woman actually broke you, remember? You were forced into womanhood before you were even a woman, Vuyiseka. By your uncle. And you spoke up about that too. You were loud about it even though the neighbours sneered, and the police dismissed your claims. "Sexual violence", "rape", "molestation" — you named the ways in which your uncle broke the yolk of your womanhood before your time. You painted your body white and smeared the streets with your blood when that happened. Why did you do that, Vuyiseka? How could you do that? Where did you get the strength and courage to make your voice heard even when the world tried to paralyse your vocal cords?

"Artists!" My mother scoffed with hatred dense in her trembling voice at people like you. You wondered why I stopped playing with you, Vuyiseka. It was because of my mother. She warned me that you would corrupt me with your volcanic temper and tantrums, your loud emotions and radical ideas, your paintbrushes, and those strokes of artistic blood.

She was wrong, I realise now. I would have found the courage to embrace my womanhood sooner had I stuck around. But my mother — she was a woman too.
An older woman trying to navigate her body as best as she knew how.

If I were to choose between your way of womaning and my mother's way, I'd lose myself, Vuyiseka. I have to find what works for me.

SHAME

i have soiled myself
because of the fear
of living with this man
as a woman

i have soiled myself
because i am a woman
in this land
whose soil is sown with seeds of patriarchy

i soiled myself
when i heard his footsteps approaching
then his hoarse voice echoing
in the house

i soiled myself
when his coarse hands touched my body
without consent
his claws digging into my vagina

he took what was never his
and left me with all this
shame
of having soiled myself

JUST F**CKING

I spiralled.
I lost myself and hated everything about my existence
the day my lover woke up with unforgiving amnesia.

He forgot
   everything!

He forgot all that he had pretended to be the previous
night. His brain must have packed the props he had put
on to pose as a genuine lover while we slept with our
bodies intertwined after sex.

He forgot how he showered me with unsolicited love while
I undressed my fragility.

He forgot how he sedated me with cheap wine,
passionate kisses, and convincing lust we picked up at
the bar that night.

He forgot how his lips and tongue traced lines between
my thighs and located him to the folds of my vagina.

He forgot how we fucked, screamed, moaned, and dug
our claws into each other's backs.

He forgot how he made promises to be more than a passing fling without saying it.

He marked his intentions with erotic strokes.
Men are supposed to stay after making love to a woman like that.

He forgot the most important rule of **just fucking**:
Never tell a desperate girl, you just met, you love her while making love to her.

"It was nice meeting you," with a haughty smile, he picked up bits of himself from the floor in the morning and fled the scene of my body's ruination.

A BLEEDING WOUND

Outside a shack, Zanzi sits with her legs spread wide. Between them is a bucket filled with dirty water, two large steel pots, and a sunlight bar soap. She hums a sorrowful tune as she scrubs one of the pots with steel-wool. Zanzi's face is weary, making her seem like a woman carrying the burdens of the entire township.

Bathandile walks into the yard carrying a bundle of painted canvases tucked under his left arm. He walks slowly with a hunched back and defeat heavy on the soles of his feet.

As Bathandile approaches their shack and draws near to Zanzi, he clears his throat. She senses his presence, stopping her humming, but keeps her gaze fixed on the pot she is scrubbing.

The tension from their recent argument lingers heavily in the air, almost tangible between them.

"Zanzi," Bathandile murmurs, his voice barely audible.

Zanzi keeps scrubbing the pot, acting as if she didn't hear him.

"Zanzi, I'm sorry about earlier," he says again, his tone laced with regret.

This time, she stops scrubbing, pausing for a moment, her frustration evident in the way she sighs.

"Did you sell anything today?" Zanzi asks, steering clear of the subject of their recent fight, which had centred on money.

Bathandile stays silent. Zanzi finally looks up at him, only to see him shake his head in hopelessness. Disappointment joins the sadness already etched on her face. She returns to scrubbing the pot, but her strokes are more forceful now, driven by anger.

Bathandile sets the bundled canvases on the ground and takes a seat beside Zanzi.

"Things are not going well in town, sthandwa sami," he says softly, almost as if he is afraid his words might ignite her rage.

Zanzi snaps anyways, abruptly putting down the pot and steel-wool.

"Hee! Do you think I am blind? You think I can't see that things are not going well, Bathandile?"

"No, Zanzi. I—"

"Do you think I am stupid? Anyone can see that things aren't going well! Even the neighbours know about our situation now. Do I look blind to you?" Her voice is like burning coal.

He lowers his head, regretting that he spoke. These days, anything sets his woman off — his calm and low voice, his breathing, his art, his presence, his unemployment, his very existence. Everything seems to be a trigger.

Zanzi cuts off her rant...

The silence between them is heavy.

Bathandile looks down at her bruised hands.

"I think it's my thoughts that have manifested this reality, Za. I haven't been okay since that…" He trails off, staring into the distance. "I think I need to see a therapist. I need help."

Zanzi chuckles derisively, then stands and moves away from him.

"Therapy? Therapy, Bathandile?" Her voice is louder than before. "Are we going to eat your emotions and this therapy of yours? Your damn art can barely feed us, and you want to waste even more time talking to a stranger about our troubles when you should be out there finding work. What is your problem? Do you enjoy it when the neighbours laugh at us, at me?"

"You don't understand." He stands and takes a step toward her.

"What is it that I don't understand? That you had one bad thing happen to you, and now we all have to suffer for it? Why are you so weak? How are you so soft for a man?"

"Why are you so stubbornly strong?!" he shouts, his rage boiling over.

Zanzi is stunned by his outburst, her expression shifting to one of hurt. His words feel like a dagger to her heart. Her eyes widen, then begin to gloss with tears.

"Life is suffering, Bathandile." Her voice is softer than before, but the pain is unmistakeable.

"Do you think that night didn't affect me just as much as it did you? Do you think I don't hurt inside?" Tears stream down her cheeks. "I suffer too, but I can't show it because the world tells us that as black women, *siyizimbokodo*. But to tell you the truth, Bathandile, **I am a bleeding wound**."

With more rage than before, Zanzi bends to pick up her bucket. She stuffs the pots and steel-wool into it, then storms into the house, leaving her husband to confront the brutal realisation that his wife bears more of a burden than she ever lets on.

FATHER'S HOMECOMING

The last ounce of frustration drained from his body as he pointed the gun at his mother and, with little hesitation, pulled the trigger, shooting her in the head. The gun had belonged to his father — the only thing he had left to remember him by. In a moment of intense but fleeting disappointment, frustration and anger directed at his father's abandonment, he had burnt all his father's clothes, thrown out his music notes, and given away his shoes. The gun was the only thing he kept, with no intention of ever using it...

It was not hate that made him kill his mother and her lover, but desperation, a venomous desperation, as he longed for his father to come back home.

He sat down in the pool of blood that oozed from his mother's head, her lifeless body sprawled beside him. Oh, how he loved her! He told himself he did this for her, for his father, and the dignity of their family. He believed he was preserving the honour of a once-beautiful, once-envied union. He wanted to reclaim the image of their family from a time when it was still respected. She had become what he despised most in women: a drunkard and a township bus that every man who lacked self-respect rode. No, this was not his father's wife. This was not his mother! She was not the woman who raised him, not the woman he wanted his estranged, musician father to come back to. He knew his father would never come back as long as she lived like this. The rumours about her reckless behaviour and could have reached his ears and kept him away all this time. No man wanted a whore for a wife, and no boy wanted a drunkard for a mother.

When he pulled the trigger, he felt neither remorse nor guilt. The woman had changed so much that she was unrecognisable to him. To him, he was not killing his mother but a stranger inhabiting his mother's body. He felt a sense of pride and relief. The stranger, the woman who drank everyday from morning till night, roamed the streets, danced in taverns with boys his age, invited them into his father's sheets and spent his father's money, was finally gone. He hoped that this would bring his father back. It had been five long years since his father left, and he was desperate for things to return to the way they were.

He laid on his mother's ballooned and bare chest. She was naked, and so was the 20-year-old boy who lay beside her body. He had shot the boy first. When he closed his eyes, he imagined his father — proud, lively and energetic — walking through the door, strumming his guitar. A faint smile tugged at the corner of his lips. His father would soon return. At least, that was his hope.

THE GOOD WIFE

All you remember is waking up at dawn to pick up the shattered pieces of yourself left behind from last night's dance when your skin danced to the songs of his fists. You didn't cry during the dance, but you mopped the floor with your tears the next morning. You rose early to clean up the evidence and make sure that he didn't wake up to the chaos of his own making. He'd lose his temper, again, if he woke up to the mess and chaos, you feared. So, as always, you hid himself from himself to save yourself from him. You are such a good wife, Andiswa.

NIGHT RITUAL

Last night's dinner was stale, and the freezing air was merciless; it cut through me like a knife, chilling me to the bone. The night felt darker and lonelier than I had ever experienced it. He didn't come home. Not until this morning. I waited, watching the food grow cold, my feet and fingers stiff with cold.

For the first time since we married six years ago and made our home here in South Africa, I had to have dinner alone. It was our nightly ritual—the two of us, having dinner behind our shack, under the veranda. Each night after eating, we would wait for the smoke from our *mbawula* to settle before heading into our shelter with it to stay warm. There, we would dream about the future and reflect on the harsh realities of our past. We would talk until we fell asleep or, sometimes, just sit quietly, lost in our individual worlds.

But none of that happened last night. He broke our sacred ritual. He didn't come home! I stayed up all night, waiting for him to return.

I was fuming, convinced he was with that woman. I knew he adored her and had continued to visit her even after I discovered their affair. She had borne him a child—a son, an heir, something I could never give him. I wasn't surprised that he couldn't stop loving her. The child bound them together, and I couldn't deny that. But I could look the other way and pretend that he still loved me, loved me more than he loved her. Pretend that nothing was happening. Pretend the woman and her son didn't exist. After all, we were bound by something stronger than love or a cherished son. Our marriage endured for so many years because it was built on a foundation of deep, dark, and vile secrets. That's why my confidence that he would never leave me remained unshaken, until last night, when fear crept in and kept me awake. I was terrified that he had missed our ritual to be with her. If that were true, it would mean I wasn't his number one anymore. It would mean our home was crumbling down, and he no longer cared enough to prop it up with pretence, to act like everything was normal, unchanged. To act like he still loved me. It would have meant that the other woman and her son had taken my place and infiltrated our home, rendering the history and secrets that had once defined our love seem trivial.

But that wasn't the case. When he walked in this morning, I was assured that nothing had torn us apart. Our home still stood strong. Our marriage was safe. His eyes revealed what had happened, even before I took in the rest of his appearance. His tattered clothes, bruised body, swollen face, and the blood seeping from his chest and knee confirmed what I had suspected the moment I saw his weary eyes.

"Pai!" I cried as he limped and dragged himself toward me, balancing against our zinc wall, which was lined with newspapers.

"Ohhh Pai!" I leaped from the bed and rushed to him.

He fell into my arms, his weight pressing down on my frail body.

I knelt on the cold floor and cradled his head on my knees.

"Martha..." Blood spurted from his mouth when he whispered my name, trying to keep his heavy eyes open. I felt a tear roll down on my cheek. I was weaker than he was.

"I am sorry I missed dinner," He coughed. I hushed him, stroking his head and staring at his once-beautiful, black face, now battered and bloody. Then he slowly shut his eyes and fell into a chilling silence.

"I forgive you," I whispered, kissing his forehead gently, as if I might hurt him if I wasn't careful.

The world around me fell into a dead silence, just like my Pai. The painful reality set in that we'd never share dinner under the veranda again. But I found some solace in knowing that he hadn't missed dinner the previous night because of that woman. I always feared that each dinner might be our last, which is why I cherished every meal with Pai. I had a sense that one day someone would uncover that our home and marriage were built on lies, secrets, and all manner of darkness. The people who attacked Pai must have found out that he was the one who raped and murdered that girl. They probably now know that I knew all along and still chose to protect him and our marriage. I'll be far from South Africa by the time they discover that the girl's body was buried right where we built our shack.

A REAL MAN

The previous night had seen heavy rain, but by morning, the sun was peeking out from behind the dispersing storm clouds. He predicted it would be a sunny yet muddy day as he ended his 30-minute phone call with the love of his life. His broad smile softened the ruggedness of his muscular and scarred face. The conversation had him blushing and rambling in the endearing way lovers often do. They planned to meet later that evening, and he envisioned a long and happy marriage with her. He saw her as his future wife and the mother of his many children, ideally boys. After all, a real man always wants male heirs. They had only been together for two weeks, but he was already sure about her. He was ready to send a letter of *Amalobola* to her family and offer her father as many cows as he asked for. She was the perfect wife, and a real man wouldn't let a woman like her slip through his fingers. He'd felt equally certain about the last two women he dated, until they turned out to be cheeky and disobedient, especially Makhosi, who would go out with her ratchet friends without informing him. She always cried that he was **controlling, possessive and abusive** when he fetched her from wherever she was. Esihle was better to the former. The only problem with her was that she often took her time to answer his phone calls and wouldn't call him back immediately after noticing the missed calls. He would have set her straight if he had been given enough time, but she broke up with him and filed a restraining order after he slapped her. She called him a **misogynist**. None of that mattered to him anymore. He had finally found his "sweet bird", a woman who flattered his male ego perfectly. Nomasonto was the quiet, unquestioning and docile type. She was always available when he called. *"Wum'kami lo.* This is my wife," he often thought to himself with pride.

At 8.a.m, he stepped into his father's backyard and opened the kraal.

1, 2, 3...18, 19, 20....35. He always counted the cattle before leading them out of the kraal to graze each morning and evening. He led, and the cows followed. If any of them wandered off in a different direction, he used his whip to steer them back onto his chosen path. Whether leading from the front or the back, he always had his whip, and his father's cows followed. This was the same approach he expected from his women. He led the cattle out of the kraal and through the yard, down into the valley, and toward the river. There, he paused for a few minutes to let the cows drink, then guided them to the open fields of Kwam'dansane, where they grazed on the dry yet plentiful grass. He let the cattle graze in the field for as long as his rumination and daydreaming permitted each time. On that sunny but muddy morning, the cows grazed for longer than usual because his rumination ran long. He was lost in thought, staring out at the mountains, when a young girl with a well-built frame and a slim waist walked by, carrying a plastic bag filled with bananas and apples. She was captivating! The tight pencil skirt she wore accentuated her figure, highlighting her curves and her silhouette. Observing her physique, he believed she exuded a sense of abundant fertility, which excited his manhood. He whistled at her, just as he often did with his herd of cows. But she ignored him and kept walking. So he called out to her as one would to another person, saying, "*Sawubona sisi! Sawubona sisi!*" (Hello sister! Hello sister!). Still, she continued on. "*Yima lapho phela!*" (Please wait there!). He hurried after her, yet she walked as if unaware of him. Her perceived arrogance and persistent indifference didn't anger him at first, because he believed it was the nature of all women to initially avoid what they desired. He thought they ran from their pursuers, even when secretly wanting to be caught, both for the thrill of the chase and to test how much the pursuer truly wanted them.

"Most of the time, when a woman says no, what she really means is yes," his uncles had taught him.

So, he persisted and followed her.

Her short legs made long strides, but he eventually caught up with her, almost out of breath. *"Sawubona, nkosazana,"* (Hello, princess,) he greeted with a smile, positioning himself in front of her to block her path. The girl stopped in her tracks, nodded at him, moved to the side, and then kept walking. He could tell she wasn't from the area by the mask she was wearing. Only city people wore masks because they were the only ones who believed the virus was real. This girl, who wore a mask and carried herself with an air of arrogance, was definitely from the city. She showed a distinct lack of interest and an air of arrogance. He'd never been rejected or ignored by a woman like that before, especially after he had smiled so charmingly. The girl's quickened pace confirmed her disinterest. He didn't stand a chance. The harsh rejection bruised his ego, stirring up a wave of unjustified animosity and frustration within him. He felt an intense urge to grab her and pin her to the ground. He despised her type—the haughty city women who looked down on men from the village. Fuelled by this hatred, he rushed after her and acted on his misogynistic instincts. In no time, the girl was on the muddy ground, wrestling against his body and screaming as he mounted her forcefully. He struggled as he lifted her skirt, trying to keep her pinned to the ground while forcing her thighs apart. She wailed and groaned in agony as he violently inserted himself inside her, pleasuring himself. When he was finished, her sobs had turned into muffled whispers, and she lay still. He zipped up his cargo pants, knelt beside her body, and gave her a sly, self-satisfied grin. He moved even closer to remove her mask, his intense vitality and pride diminished on the spot when he did. His scream was like that of a hen having its throat slit as he recoiled in shock. He scrambled to his feet and backed away, studying the girl from a distance. She bore an uncanny resemblance to the woman he loved. This girl, whom he had pinned to the mound of wet dirt with violent force, splitting her thighs apart to violate her private parts, was the splitting image of his Nomasonto.

At that moment, he recalled that Nomasonto had once vaguely mentioned that she had a deaf younger sister who lived and studied in the city. This girl could be his beautiful lover's sister, he realised. She was! She was just as striking and as well-built as Nomasonto. A surge of fear and panic gripped him as he stared at her. What would happen when his family and Nomasonto's became one, and this girl recognised him? She would reveal the darkness of his true character, exposing the vileness within him. His head reeled with dizziness. He glanced around frantically, and his darting eyes settled on a rock lying beside the girl's brutalized body. He picked it up, bent over her body, and smashed it against her head. Blood spilled on the rock, her face and his shirt...

Only the sky, the wet dirt, the grass, the mountains, and his father's cows would know what transpired on that sunny yet muddy morning. He needed to protect his relationship at all costs. Later, he would see his lover, ready to offer comfort for her loss—after all, that's what a "real man" does when his future wife loses her sister.

TADANA

The air was pregnant with silence after it happened, a silence saturated with fear and grief. Flies buzzed around her mutilated, lifeless body. A bare body laid on the blood-soaked streets for the whole world to gasp in horror, pity, and shame at. Her torn clothes exposed her open, bleeding wounds. She bled to death on those streets. No one dared to call the police or summon an ambulance as she struggled against him for her life, even as she took her last breath. They didn't call, not only because they feared him, but also because she wasn't one of them. She was an outcast, a pariah, unworthy of their help in their eyes. Her violently spread thighs and torn underwear exposed her shredded woman parts. The sight was revolting; she looked undesirable.

It was exactly what he wanted.

Tadana was a twenty-three-year-old lady who had relocated to this part of the country to pursue her studies. A hostile township! But this place was far better to occupy than to waste her youth, her brains, and beauty in the bundus, where her family came from. It was closer to the city, where she was studying and also gave her proximity to an abundance of opportunity. Had she stuck around for longer, lived until maybe twenty-four or twenty-five, I believe she could have afforded to move from the shabby backroom she rented in the township to a nice, high-end apartment in the city. A rich blesser would have paid for it, but she didn't play her cards right. She wasn't smart enough to pick the right man, unlike most of my girls and me. We all made sure to pick a perfectly miserable and rich old man—but not her. The whole point of dating a sugar daddy when you still have your youthful bosom and heavenly beauty to flaunt around is to gain financial freedom... Well, maybe not freedom, but financial uhmm... I can't think of the word right now. Not independence either, but to have the luxury, the money, and the glamorous lifestyle so many naive and clueless girls covet on social media, you know? It's pointless—and even foolish—to date someone much older if they don't have money to offer. A sugar daddy has to have "sugar". Tadana's daddy didn't, though. So, he wasn't even a sugar daddy. He was a struggling, broke and dangerous car mechanic with a wife and three kids. He lived far from where she stayed, but his mechanic shop was situated in the same yard where she rented her backroom. That's where they met. I get so irritated just thinking about what Tadana was even doing with a man like that. A whole mechanic!? Not even a tavern or a taxi owner, at least.

But a man who fixes other men's broken cars, counts pennies and wears greasy overalls from Monday to Sunday. Ugh!

They had been seeing each other for no more than three months when Tadana found out about the wife and the kids. She didn't seem to mind, though. She told me that she was not looking for a long-term commitment at that point. Yet, from the way she talked about him, it was clear she was head over heels in love. He was all she ever spoke about when we met for our day-drinking sessions with friends. It's not important how she and I became friends. I only want to briefly tell you about her affair with that car mechanic of hers before painting a vivid picture of her gruesome murder.

A gory scene!

Since they were in the same space almost everyday, they spent a lot of time together—more than with anyone else —and grew fond of each other, forming a solid bond. Despite their bond, I always felt that there were too many cracks in their relationship. The man was a walking red flag. Yes, I understand that having a sugar daddy is frowned upon in our society and often considered immoral, even seen as a red flag. But what are the options for a young woman in a country plagued by unemployment and inequality? At the end of the day, you have to eat, and morality doesn't pay the bills. And besides, most sugar daddies are actually sweet and kind, if I'm being honest. They treat us much better than guys our own age. But Tadana's man... he was nothing like a sugar daddy, despite being older. He didn't treat her right, nor did he ease her financial burdens. This guy had Tadana cooking him lunch and dinner, yet he never, not once, bothered to buy her groceries or give her money. All he did was take, take, take and mistreat her.

He hit her once, I remember. She never told me about it, but I saw it with my own eyes. The bruises and marks on her body were a tell-tale of how he had been turning her body into a scene of violence months before he killed her. It frustrates me just thinking about it! Why didn't she walk away? Why did she end up returning home as a corpse instead of leaving after the first slap!? That's something I'll never understand because I was never brave enough to ask her.

Even before the physical abuse, the relationship revealed itself as an emotionally taxing and toxic situation. Tadana once came to me in absolute shock, her body trembling and tears streaming down her face ceaselessly. She only told me that he had shared something dangerous about himself during their pillow-talk, after she had fed him and satisfied his whims, of course. Apparently, he had shared something she felt she could never digest or forgive. She seemed shattered by the confession. She didn't tell me what he had admitted to, and I didn't ask—she couldn't bring herself to say it. From the fear that loomed in her eyes when she came to me, I thought she would end their affair, or that perhaps she had already done so. However, to my surprise and disappointment, she was back in his arms just a few nights later, choosing to "look past his flaws and the horror of his confession".

I believe that the signs that the affair would end badly for her were always there. That incident was one of them—a glaring red flag. Yet, she chose to ignore them. And I let her.

Shortly after that red flag—the confession—things went from bad to worse. The slaps and punches, once delivered in secret, escalated to a brutal attack carried out in broad daylight with an audience. I don't think he was thinking straight that day. His anger must have been so intense that he forgot to hide from the world that he wasn't only a cheater, sleeping with someone the same age as her daughter, but that he was also an abuser. A man who resolved his romantic affairs with fists. A man who couldn't control his temper. A man who threw deadly tantrums when he was betrayed, as if he weren't already betraying his wife. This shift happened because a few weeks before Tadana's fatal assault, she found a real boyfriend—someone her age, who didn't come with all the baggage and red flags that the car mechanic came with. She was planning to break up with the car mechanic but said she needed some time. I was relieved to hear that she was finally ready to walk away from the toxic relationship. She just needed to summon the courage to tell him. But now, after everything that has happened— after her murder—I doubt breaking up with him would have changed her fate, unless she moved away from the township immediately after breaking the news. I think he would have killed her for leaving him. He was too attached, possessive, and controlling.

He didn't actually see them together to start accusing her of "cheating," but he noticed a change in her moods and behaviour around him—her reduced availability and suddenly busy schedule. It was enough for him to assume that there was someone else. It's easy for cheaters to recognise the signs that they are no longer their lover's only romantic interest. I laughed when she told me that he accused her of cheating and was filled with rage because of it. I laughed because of the absurdity of their relationship. Wasn't he a cheater himself? Wasn't she his side-chick? That's the problem with men—they can't stomach half of the cruel things they do to women. Can you imagine a man staying with a woman for years knowing she has a husband and kids? Can you imagine a man dating a woman with multiple partners but is asked that he only sees one woman? Can you imagine a man with a possessive, obsessive, and abusive woman? Can you imagine a man enduring the torture, trauma, and turmoil women face throughout their lifetimes because of men? No man could withstand it. Tadana's car mechanic was no different.

He became more aggressive when he began to suspect that she was seeing someone else. He turned into a violent brute. The day he turned her body into stone, the day he made her life a memory, was the day after she had spent the night away—at her real boyfriend's place. He had called her excessively throughout the night and even slept in the yard, in one of the cars he was fixing, waiting for her to come back. She didn't return until the following morning, by which time he had turned into a raging forest fire, completely uncontrollable.

Tadana got burned the minute she walked into the yard. He unleashed venomous insults when he laid eyes on her. He followed her inside her room, continuing his verbal tirade once they were inside.

I wasn't there when the gory scene unfolded, but the tenants who rented rooms in the same yard painted a vivid picture for me. They said that once Tadana and her car mechanic were inside the room, the insults were accompanied with what sounded like punches. Then they heard her piercing screams and the thud of her hitting a wall. They listened the way one listens to a tragic tale on the radio, imagining how everything played out behind those closed doors.

They didn't intervene for several reasons, according to them:

1. They believed a neighbour shouldn't get involved in a dispute between lovers.
2. They feared the car mechanic more than anyone else in the township.
3. They didn't care about Tadana.
4. They had grown accustomed to their fighting.

Given those reasons, they carried on with their lives as if a young woman wasn't suffering at the hands of an unscrupulous older man. They thought it would end soon, as it usually did, but it didn't. Before they knew it, they heard the sound of glass breaking. Tadana climbed out through the shattered window, trying to escape from her own backroom—one she paid for herself. The shards of glass cut into her flesh as she climbed out. He burst out of the room, chasing her with a screwdriver in hand. He shouted at her like a madman, hurling insults, diminishing her dignity with every step. The commotion drew the neighbours out of their houses. Even those who were already outside when she made her escape just stood by and watched, as did those who came out because of the noise. Despite Tadana's desperate pleas for help, no one intervened. They kept their distance, watching in pity, horror, or shame.

When he caught up with her, he attacked from behind, pinning her to the ground, and began digging the screwdriver into her flesh. Her screams tore through the air as she fought for her last breaths. Even then, no one stepped in to save her. Blood gushed from her mouth as she sobbed her final sobs. When he had had enough of digging the screwdriver into her flesh, he ripped her underwear to expose her private parts to bring shame to her dying body. I think he must have believed that this act of cruelty would somehow compensate for the humiliation he felt when he found out he was no longer her only lover.

Tadana died a brutal and merciless death at the hands of a monster, while a passive audience looked on. I can't help but wonder how many other women have died at the hands of their lovers, with society staying silent or turning a blind eye.

A Book of Prose, Monologues & Short Stories

This literary masterpiece delves deep into the nuanced experiences of women, peeling back layers to reveal the profound impacts of gender-based violence, sexual abuse, generational trauma, and the intricate web of challenges inherent in traversing the terrain of womanhood within the rigid confines of a patriarchal societal structure. Through richly textured narratives and profound insights, it illuminates the myriad complexities, struggles, and resilience of different female characters as they navigate a world shaped by unequal power dynamics and entrenched gender norms.

ABOUT THE WRITER

Okuhle Esethu, legally known as Lindokuhle Esethu
Hlatshwayo, is a visionary creative writer and editor with
a rich background in literature, film, and drama.
She holds a Bachelor of Arts degree
in Communications and Media and English Literature
from the University of Johannesburg,
along with an Honours degree
in English Literature with a Scriptwriting minor
from the University of Cape Town.
As an accomplished author, she has written and
published seven books, each one a testament to her
exceptional talent and dedication to her craft.
Armed with a deep understanding of storytelling
conventions, she fearlessly breaks the rules to ignite
creativity in her writing.

www.ingramcontent.com/pod-product-compliance
Lightning Source LLC
Chambersburg PA
CBHW030346030726
47499CB00003B/928